GEORGE THE WOMBAT

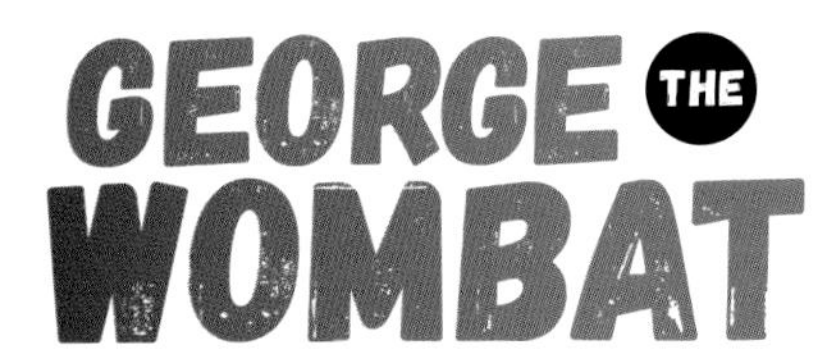

Woodslane Press Pty Ltd
10 Apollo Street
Warriewood, NSW 2102
Email: info@woodslane.com.au
Tel: 02 8445 2300 **Website:** www.woodslanepress.com.au

First published in Australia in 2023 by Woodslane Press

Royalties from the sale of this book go to support Aussie Ark, a not-for-profit organisation dedicated to wildlife conservation.

Original text and publishing consultant Jo Runciman

Design Mike Ellott

A catalogue record for this book is available from the National Library of Australia

Printed in Malaysia by Times International Printing

Cover image: George the Wombat

Wombats are Australian **marsupials**. This means they are **warm-blooded** and they have pouches to carry their babies (**joeys**) in.

Wombats live in **burrows**. They dig burrows using their powerful claws.

Wombats' pouches face backwards. This is so a mother wombat can dig without her **pouch** filling up with dirt.

This is the story of **George**, an **orphan wombat** joey. George was raised by keepers at **The Australian Reptile Park.**

Poor little **George the Wombat** became an orphan after his mum was hit by a car.

Lucky for George, the kind person who found his mum checked her **pouch**.

Inside, she found little George – unhurt!

Carefully, she took George out of his mum's pouch.

Then she took him to **The Australian Reptile Park** to be cared for by **experts**.

When George first arrived, he had only light, **velvety** fur.

This was not enough to keep him warm.

So, **Tim** became George's main carer.

Being a **wombat carer** is a tough job!

Tim had to get up a lot during the night to check on George.

He had to feed him and give him lots of cuddles – just like a newborn baby.

TIM

Tim made George a **woollen pouch** to sleep in.

At first, George was very **shy** and **stubborn!**

He did not want to come out of his **pouch**.
He did not want to drink his milk.

Tim tried again and again.

But stubborn George bit on his bottle.
His special **marsupial milk** went everywhere!

Everyone was very worried as George
needed to drink to **survive**.

Finally, **George** got so hungry
he couldn't resist the milk.

Once he got the hang of drinking from
a bottle, he didn't want to stop!

George became a little piggy and
he **gained weight** fast.

At mealtimes, he poked his nose out of
his woollen pouch, waiting for his bottle.

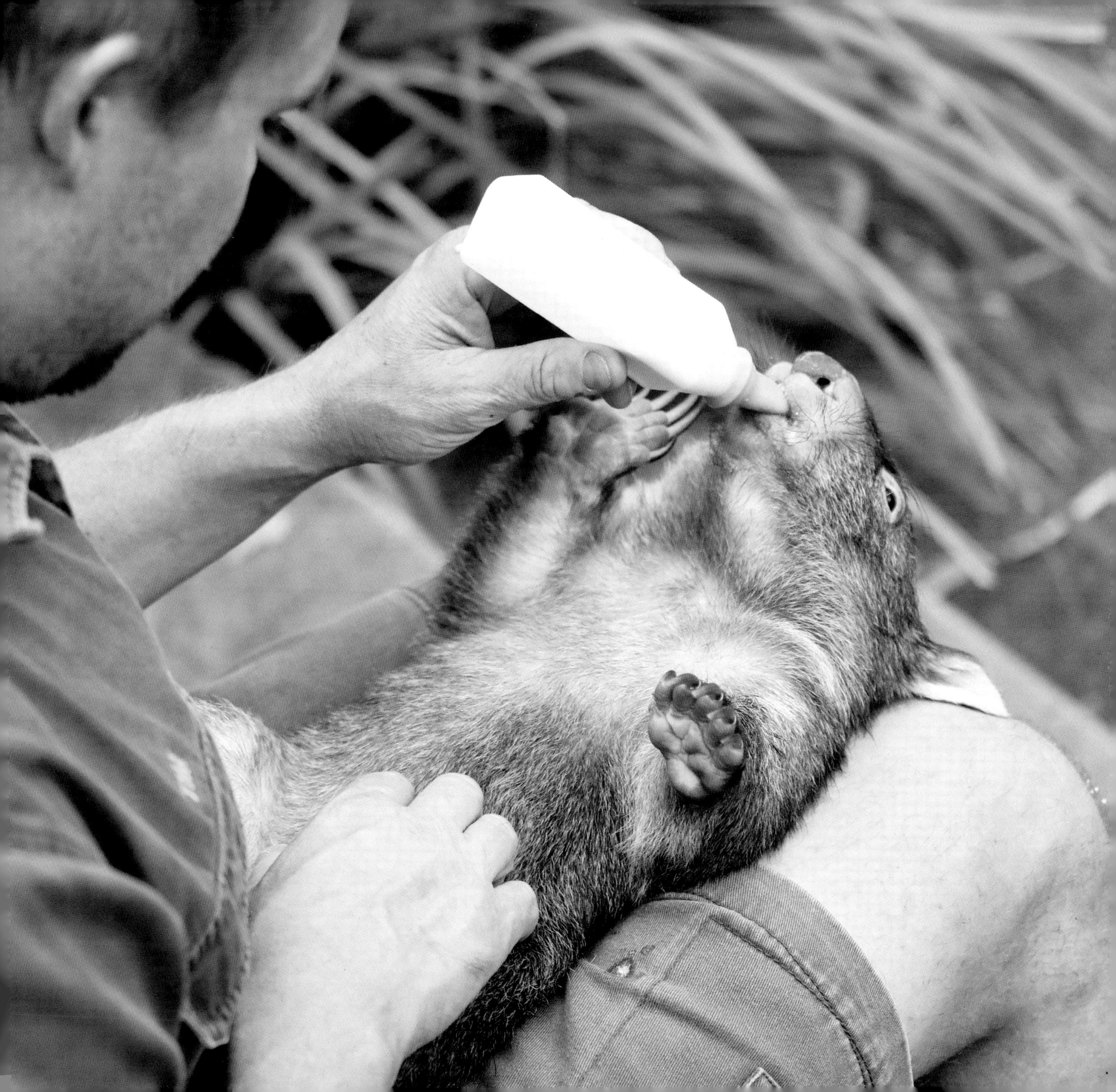

George absolutely loved **Tim**.

Other than sleeping and eating, having a cuddle with Tim was his favourite thing to do.

Tim made George a new bed in a **chest of drawers.**

This became George's **favourite place**.

When **George** was tired, he took himself off to bed.

He usually slept **on his back**, with his four little legs sticking up in the air!

Sometimes, in the middle of the night, he tried to climb into bed with **Tim**!

10

As **George** got older, he tried to always be right between **Tim's** legs – just like he would have been with his mum **in the wild**.

Wherever **Tim** went, **George** followed.

As George grew, he started eating **solid food** – just like he would have done in the wild.

The first solid food he ate was **dried grass** and **lucerne**.

Slowly, he tried **vegetables** and fresh, **green grass**.

His favourite food was **roots** with lots of dirt which ended up EVERYWHERE!

George became very cheeky and playful.

He loved running away with **Tim's** slippers.

Tim played **zoomies** with George as he tried to catch him.

Wombats love to play **zoomies** – just like dogs love to chase balls.

Tim brought George to **The Australian Reptile Park** every day.

He got to know the other **keepers**, and everyone fell in love with him.

George's sweet, funny nature made him everyone's favourite.

AUSTRALIAN
REPTILE
PARK

George loved having his belly scratched and he loved to chase the keepers.

From a shy stubborn little boy, **George** turned into a friendly, **bossy**, happy grown-up.

As he got older, the keepers at **The Australian Reptile Park** knew it was time for **George** to go back **into the wild**.

After being raised by humans, it is a big **challenge** for wombats to go back **into the wild**.

Luckily, **The Australian Reptile Park** has a special place to **release orphan animals** like George.

Here, they can roam like wild **native animals**, but they are given extra support.

Food is left out for them and, if they need to, they can come back.

George is now a happy, healthy adult wombat.

He lives in the **bush**.

But he still sneaks back for a sweet potato treat sometimes!

WOMBAT FACTS

DESCRIPTION

The common wombat has short, rounded ears, a large, hairless nose, and coarse, thick fur.

Wombats have powerful, strong claws for digging burrows.

Their pouches open to the rear, so they don't fill with soil while they are digging.

Their rump is protected by a bony plate that acts as a shield. They use this part of their bodies to block their burrows to keep predators out.

Wombats are big, solid animals and adults can weigh over 30 kilograms.

In summer, they are mostly nocturnal. In winter, when it is not as hot, they will come out during the day.

Wombats do share their burrows with other wombats but usually only one is home at a time.

Although they are not territorial in where they sleep, they are territorial about feeding areas.

They scent mark their feeding territories and defend them aggressively.

Wombats come in different shades of grey and brown, depending on where they live.

A group of wombats is called a wisdom.

Wombats prefer the forests of temperate south-eastern Australia, including alpine areas.

They also inhabit coastal habitats and heathland.

They live in burrows, which can be up to 20 metres long with several burrow systems they use at different times.

Wombats prefer to dig their burrows in the slopes above creeks, to prevent them flooding.

WATCH GEORGE!

Scan the QR code to see a video of George at **The Australian Reptile Park**

GLOSSARY

alpine: high, mountain region

bony plate: round piece of bone

burrow: a hole in the ground to live or shelter in

carer: someone who takes care of someone or something

challenge: a contest of skill and strength

coarse: harsh or rough to touch

coastal: of or at a coast

expert: someone with a special skill or knowledge

forage: to look for food

habitat: where a plant or animal naturally lives or grows

heathland: open land covered in low green shrubs

joey: a baby wombat, koala, kangaroo, quoll, possum, and other marsupials

keeper: someone whose job it is to look after animals

lucerne: a plant with bluish purple flowers

mange: skin disease due to parasitic mites

marsupials: animals with a pouch or fold of skin on the abdomen of the females (contains mammary glands and serves to house and feed their babies)

native animal: descended from original inhabitants of a country

nocturnal: active at night

orphan: with no parents

pouch: a fold of skin on the abdomen of female marsupials (contains mammary glands and serves to house and feed their babies)

predator: a hunter or killer

roots: part of a plant that fixes it under the soil and absorbs water and nutrients

scent mark: to rub up against and leave a smell that marks their territory

shield: defensive equipment

shy: easily frightened

stubborn: fixed or set in purpose

survive: to remain alive

temperate: moderate temperature, not too hot or too cold

territorial: defence of territory

territory: an area of land

the wild: free natural habitat

velvety: smooth and soft

warm-blooded: having a constant body temperature

zoomies: when some animals run in an excited way that seems to have no purpose